FOUR SEASONS of FUN
Egg Hunts! Fireworks! Pumpkins! Reindeer!

By Pamela Duncan Edwards and Illustrated by Sylvie Daigneault

Glittering sunbeams make a golden crown
for a tree that is wearing a blossom gown.

Out from a burrow two black eyes peep;
groundhog has finished his winter sleep.

It's **spring** and soon you'll be...

Skipping, jumping, hearing friends cheer,
Running, shouting, "Sunny days are here!"

Flying a kite, watching it dive,
Seeing it wheel as if it's alive.

Hunting in ponds to find pollywogs,
Marveling that tadpoles turn into frogs.

Listening for the patter of bunny feet,
Wondering if he'll leave you a candy treat.

Hearing the birds as they warble and sing,

Tweeting love to their mates because it is spring.

Shimmering now in leafy green,
the tree stands tall, a royal queen,

Sheltering a nest where babes lie snug,
beaks reaching up for a tasty bug.

It's **summer** and soon you'll be…

Chasing butterflies and hiding in trees,
Racing downhill and grazing your knees.

Fishing, hiking, with rocks to climb,
Calling, "LEMONADE! A CUP FOR A DIME!"

Setting up for your barbecue,
Working as part of the serving crew.

Honoring your nation as fireworks soar,

Gasping and clapping and shouting for more.

Splashing in pools, hitting a run,
Slam-dunking a ball—summer is fun.

Whispering secrets to the soft wind blowing,
the tree rustles and dances, yellow leaves glowing.

With gray tail quivering, a squirrel races,
burying nuts in secret places.

It's **fall** and soon you'll be . . .

Riding your bike through a leafy heap,

Ringing the bell as you swerve and leap.

Racing the field, taking aim,

Helping your team to win the game.

Bundling up for a walk in the park,

Counting the stars, skipping home in the dark.

Carving a pumpkin, roasting a s'more,
Plucking up courage at the haunted house door.

Smiling, hugging, saying, "HI!"
Licking lips because **fall** means turkey and pie.

Sparkling with frost, the tree's branches are bare;
a fox lifts her snout and sniffs at the air.

Dark clouds tumble like kittens at play;
fox knows that snow is on its way.

It's **winter** and soon you'll be...

Stamping ice puddles that nip your toes,
  Building a snowman with a carroty nose.

Making snow angels, sledding down hills,
  Laughing with friends when you have spills.

Sipping hot chocolate to thaw out your bones,
Choosing the colors to paint your pinecones.

Leaving cookies for Santa, hoping he comes,

High-fiving next morning when you find crumbs.

Playing games indoors, learning to skate,
Snuggling by the fire, winter is great.

Glittering sunbeams make a golden crown
for a tree that is wearing a blossom gown.

Out from a burrow two black eyes peep;
groundhog has finished his winter sleep.

It's spring again.

For my sweet friends Emma Elizabeth and Alexandra Claire Olson.
May you find wonder in every season of the year.

With love, Pam

❧

To Tomas and Gabriel

—Sylvie

Text Copyright © 2019 Pamela Duncan Edwards
Illustration Copyright © 2019 Sylvie Daigneault
Design Copyright © 2019 Sleeping Bear Press

Sleeping Bear Press®
2395 South Huron Parkway, Suite 200
Ann Arbor, MI 48104
www.sleepingbearpress.com

Printed and bound in the United States.

10 9 8 7 6 5 4 3 2

Library of Congress Cataloging-in-Publication Data

Names: Edwards, Pamela Duncan, author. | Daigneault, Sylvie, illustrator.
Title: Four seasons of fun : egg hunts! fireworks! pumpkins! reindeer! /
written by Pamela Duncan Edwards ; illustrated by Sylvie Daigneault.
Description: Ann Arbor, MI : Sleeping Bear Press, [2018] | Summary: Rhyming text
celebrates the four seasons, emphasizing outdoor and indoor activities and holidays.
Identifiers: LCCN 2018006620 | ISBN 9781585364039
Subjects: | CYAC: Stories in rhyme. | Seasons—Fiction.
Classification: LCC PZ8.3.E283 Fo 2018 | DDC [E]—dc23
LC record available at https://lccn.loc.gov/2018006620